CAKE

For Chris Inns and Laura Roberts,
thank you for helping us to bake our little cake.

First published 2018 by Macmillan Children's Books
an imprint of Pan Macmillan
20 New Wharf Road, London N1 9RR
Associated companies throughout the world
www.panmacmillan.com

ISBN 978-1-5098-2742-8 (HB)
ISBN 978-1-5098-2743-5 (PB)
ISBN 978-1-5098-8199-4 (Ebook)

Text and Illustrations copyright © Sue Hendra and Paul Linnet 2018

1 3 5 7 9 8 6 4 2

A CIP catalogue record for this book is available from
the British Library.

Printed in China

Sue Hendra & Paul Linnet

CAKE

MACMILLAN CHILDREN'S BOOKS

Cake had just received an exciting invitation.

He'd never been to a party before,
so he didn't know what to expect.
But he was sure about one thing —
he wanted to look his best.

Fish didn't know what Cake should wear.
He'd never been to a party either.

"Hmmm . . ." said Fish.

"Nope."

"I don't think so."

"What about a hat?" suggested Fish.

"Good thinking!" said Cake.

So off Cake went to buy a hat.

Cake tried on lots of hats in the shop.

But none of them
were quite right.

"Is it for a special occasion?" asked the shop assistant. "A wedding perhaps?"

"No," said Cake, "a party."

"Oh," said the shop assistant.
"In that case, I have just the thing."

And he disappeared
out the back.

"Here you go, Sir," said the shop assistant.
"You'll be irresistible in this."

"Thank you very much,"
said Cake.

He couldn't wait to
get home and show
Fish his new hat.

"Are you ready?" Cake called from his bathroom.

"You've cracked it!" shouted Fish.

Cake was soon on his way to the party,
dressed in his new hat.

"Deedly-dee, deedly-dum, I'm off to a party to have some fun!"

Cake was a bit nervous
when he arrived.

But when everyone saw him, they cheered!
"CAKE'S HERE! A party isn't a party without
CAKE!" they said. And in he went.

Cake was having so much
fun at the party.

There was dancing,

and lots of games.

But then, the singing started . . .

"Happy birthday to you,

happy birthday to you..."

Cake was getting a bad feeling about this.

"Oh, crumbs!"

Suddenly there was a gust of wind and everything went ...

BLACK!

Then there was a smell of raspberries . . .

and Cake felt a wibbly-wobbly
hand grab hold of his . . .